I0741768

This story follows Stevie as he returns to the forest to help save the animals from the dangers of sin. With the support of his friends, Stevie shows the creatures of the forest the depth of God's love and the power of His sacrifice. Along the way, they learn and share the true meaning of love, forgiveness, and redemption.

The hour has come for the Son of Man to be glorified. As God's messengers on this earth it is our calling to share the good news. Jesus Christ died on the cross for our sins, and through faith in Him we receive everlasting life.

It had been 25 years since Stevie left the earth and went to live with Jesus and God in heaven. The animals in the forest had forgotten what Stevie had taught them and about all the miracles they had witnessed. Instead of having faith, they turned to worshipping false gods and living in sin (fighting, stealing from each other, using mean words, not helping each other, constantly complaining and being selfish).

Sassy left the forest because she was so disappointed in the animals' behavior, but Sally stayed behind so she could help save the animals. She had a family of her own now and decided to dedicate her life to teaching and supporting the animals in the forest. Sally was determined to try and make a difference in the forest and help change the animals' hearts.

Sally prayed every day and night. She prayed for God's guidance and the strength to reach the hearts of these animals. She wanted them to know that they were living in sin. Sally knew the danger of living in sin, but her desire was for every creature in the forest to live in the fullness of God's goodness and His love. She trusted that God could use her to help the animals recognize their evil ways and turn toward the light. God heard all her prayers and decided that he would help her.

Jesus also heard Sally's prayers and had a special plan for her! He chose to send Stevie back to earth to help, for Stevie might be the only one that could reach the animals. Stevie had a special story to share and his love and testimony could help the animals to understand God's love and grace.

Sally was walking through the forest one morning looking for acorns to feed her family when she saw a bright light in the corner of her eye. The light was so bright that Sally could barely see. All of a sudden she heard a familiar voice calling her name. Out of the bright light appeared Stevie just as beautiful as ever. Sally called out "Stevie, is that you?"

"Jesus sent me back to the forest to walk beside you", Stevie said softly. "He heard your prayers and knows how deeply you long to help the animals find salvation (being rescued from your sin). It is your faith and dedication that brought me here. You already have everything you need to guide the animals toward redemption (rescuing living creatures from their sin) . You have your faith, your strength, and your voice. All you need to carry is the Bible in your hands and God's love in your heart. You are ready!" Stevie's encouraging words were the words Sally needed to hear to believe in herself.

Sally was touched by the confidence Stevie had in her ability to reach the animals' hearts and share God's word with them. She longed to make a lasting impact in their lives, helping them understand the difference between right and wrong. The animals had forgotten all they once knew about God and Jesus. What they needed most was love, forgiveness, and the gift of God's grace.

Sally knew what she needed to do. She prayed that God would guide her path and show her the way. "God, please give me the wisdom and the discernment (ability to know the difference between good and evil) to understand your plan and to know how to deliver your message in a peaceful, loving, and forgiving way". She then opened up her Bible and let God guide her hands. A strong wind from the north blew and the Bible opened up to a certain page. Sally began reading God's words. She knew with God's help there was nothing that was impossible.

As Sally opened the Bible, a brilliant light from heaven shone down upon her and the Bible in her hands. Suddenly, she heard a sound like hundreds of trumpets echoing through the air. In that moment, she knew without a doubt that God was speaking directly to her. She looked at the words and read aloud Luke 23:34 "Father, forgive them, for they do not know what they are doing.

Stevie prayed with Sally so that she would not only have the faith to fulfill God's purpose in her life, but she would also have the endurance to continue to encourage, love, and forgive the animals in the forest. He knew from his experiences that you have to maintain your faith and determination to reach the animals' hearts. It would be difficult for her, but he knew she could do it! She had the vision and the faith to trust in God and allow his miracles to work in her life.

Stevie knew that God answered his prayer. Another animal had been sent to them to honor God's mission in the forest. From the grass, a young fawn stepped forward. He had been watching quietly, and now he introduced himself as Felix. Sally and Stevie warmly shared their names and explained why they were there. The animals in the forest had been living in sin, and God called them to teach His way through love, forgiveness, and the truth of His word.

Felix's eyes lit up. He told them that God had also spoken to him, asking him to join their mission and help carry out His plans. Stevie and Sally were delighted at Felix's response. They knew that God was good, and he would always help them and never forsake them. Sally said "Now I know that God will move heaven and earth to help us. With God nothing is impossible". Stevie told her that they would need to gather all the animals together.

11

Sally announced that there would be a meeting with all the animals in the forest. She asked each animal that she spoke with to spread the word. They were to all meet her in front of the large rock near the oak tree at sunset. She would inform them once everyone gathered what God had shared with her.

At first, the animals seemed very uncooperative, and she did not feel like she was presenting the message well. Then the animals saw Stevie. Several of them recognized him immediately and knew if Stevie was there then the meeting had to be very important. The animals scurried off and started sharing the message of a special meeting in front of the large rock near the oak tree. The animals were eager and curious to know more about this special message and Stevie's journey to heaven.

As Sally spoke, her voice carried great confidence. God was using her voice to speak directly with the animals in the forest. Through her, He told them that He was disappointed in their behavior, and that He had been watching them for a long time. Their disobedience and sin had brought Him deep sadness. God's voice thundered with power and authority, echoing through the trees. It was so strong and commanding that every animal listened closely and gave honor to His words.

Then Felix told the animals his story. God had spoken to him and asked him to deliver a message to the animals about their sin. He told them that God will always love them even when they do evil. He also told them that they needed to turn away from their evil ways and live a life without sin.

Stevie then added to their conversation. He told them how beautiful and wonderful heaven is and that they will have to change their ways in order to live an eternal life in heaven one day. He also said that God's love for them is special and that he will forgive them for their sins. All they have to do is ask for forgiveness and it will be given to them.

The animals gave their lives to God and Jesus that very day. They asked forgiveness for their sins and promised to live a life without evil and sin. They thanked Stevie, Sally, and Felix for their love and kindness. The animals also showed appreciation for Stevie, Sally, and Felix not giving up on them and continuing to guide them to the path of light instead of darkness. With Stevie's and Felix's help, Sally was able to reach the animals' hearts and teach them about God's love. She looked forward to many more years of dedication to helping the animals in the forest to find their way to heaven. She also knew that God and Jesus had a special plan for her life and she was just getting started. Now Stevie wondered if he would be allowed to remain in the forest or if he had to return to heaven. He realized how much work had to be done with all God's creatures and he knew where he was needed the most.

God and Jesus looked down on the animals in the forest. They were both pleased that Stevie, Sally, and Felix helped accomplish a miracle. Jesus realized that Stevie needed to stay so he could continue to fulfill his destiny. Now they have two more messengers: Sally and Felix. With God, nothing is impossible! Jesus knew that these animals could inspire many others and that they were performing miracles every day. Both God and Jesus were very pleased. They had the best servant leaders who would lead others by serving them. This is definitely the beginning of a beautiful story.......

16

Scriptures to Study:

Romans 8:31 – "If God is for us, who can be against us?"
No one can stop what God is about to do in your life.

Psalm 121:7 – "The Lord shall preserve you from all evil: He shall preserve your soul".
You might not realize it, but God blocks the devil's plans all the time.

Philippians 4:6 – "Focus on your blessings, not your struggles. Let gratitude fill you heart
for all that God has done for you.

Scriptures to Study:

Psalm 121: 7-8 "The Lord will keep you from all harm—He will watch over your life; the Lord will watch over your coming and going both now and forevermore."

Job 22:21 "Submit to God and be at peace with Him; in this way prosperity will come to you."

Isaiah 43:19 Do not lose hope in times of trouble, for God is working in the unseen. His hand is steady, and His timing is perfect in bringing good out of difficulty.

Jeremiah 29:11 "For I know the thoughts that I think toward you, said the Lord, thoughts of peace, and not of evil, to give you an expected end."

Ephesians 3:20 "Now to Him who is able to do more than all we ask or imagine, according to His power that is at work within us."

Matthew 7:7 "Ask, and it shall be given to you, seek, and you shall find; knock, and it shall be opened to you."

Luke 23:34 "Father, forgive them; for they do not know what they are doing.

About the Author

I have fallen in love with Stevie the Caterpillar and could not end his story with just one book. I decided to continue his story and to bring other characters into his narrative to teach children about love, God's grace, and forgiveness. I hope that you will love this character as much as I do and will want to share God's love and forgiveness with others. I have used Stevie as one of my examples when talking to children about the choices they are making, hoping that they will model their behavior after Stevie's behavior.

About the Author

I have been an educator in the state of Georgia for 28 years. I have always wanted to make a difference in the lives of children by teaching them and showing them how to grow into loving, helpful, and productive members of society. There is so much temptation in our world today and young people are led astray easily by what they are watching on television and seeing in video games. It is very important to me to spread God's love and His word especially among our children.

I hope you will enjoy the story of Stevie and use this book not only for entertainment purposes, but also as a bible study.

Helpful Words and Phrases:

01. Sacrifice – the act of giving up something of value to you
02. Redemption – the act of saving or being saved from sin or evil
03. Forgiveness – letting go of the person or thing that hurt you, not seeking revenge against someone who did wrong to you
04. Salvation – being saved from harm, danger, evil or sin
05. Discernment – knowing the difference between right and wrong or good and evil
06. Sin – doing the wrong thing, disobeying God
07. Faith – strong trust or belief in someone or something
08. Destiny – your future designed by something supernatural (God or Jesus)
09. The trinity – God the Father, God the Son (Jesus), and God the Holy Spirit (God's love that lives inside of us)

Stevie is on a mission to help the animals in the forest remember all of the miracles they experienced and to help them live a life without sin. His friend, Sally the Squirrel, needs his help to reach the animals' hearts and help them seek forgiveness for their sins and to live their life according to God's will.

24